TULSA CITY-COUNTY LIBRARY

D1498062

TULSA CITY-COUNTY LIBRARY

To Marie, my little Thumbelina
D. P.

To Lena and Malo
O. T.

Illustrated by
OLIVIER TALLEC

First American Edition published in 2007 by Enchanted Lion Books, 45 Main Street, Suite 519, Brooklyn, NY 11201

Originally published in French as *Poucette de Toulaba* by Rue du Monde and Daniel Picouly (text)© 2005

Translation © 2007 Enchanted Lion Books

All rights reserved. No part of this book may be reproduced, stored in a retrieval system or transmitted in any form or by any means, electronic, mechanical, photocopying recording or otherwise, without the written permission of the copyright owner, or in accordance with the provisions of the Copyright Act 1956 (as amended). Any person or persons who do any unauthorized act in relation to this publication may be liable to civil prosecution and civil claims for damages.

[A CIP record is on file with the Library of Congress]

ISBN-10: 1-59270-069-1
ISBN-13: 978-1-59270-069-1

Printed in China

2 4 6 8 10 9 7 5 3 1

Written by DANIEL PICOULY
After Hans Christian Andersen

Translated by Claudia Zoe Bedrick

Thumbelina
of Toulaba

ENCHANTED LION BOOKS
NEW YORK

Once upon a time in Toulaba, a country at the far end of far away, there lived a woman, young as the sweet breeze of spring and dark as the night when the moon merely smiles. She wanted a child, but a child no bigger than the smallest of small children. In other words, tiny. She had already had so many children that her house was full. This would be her last.

She went to see the old sorcerer who lived high at the top of a bridge of creeper vines in a wacapou tree. She asked him her question. The old sorcerer thought it over and replied:
—Take this grain of millet, a thousand times small, plant it deep as a finger in the darkest, warmest earth that you can find and you will have your little one in an instant.
The woman thanked him with twelve lemons, golden as the sun at noon. Such was the custom.

The woman set out immediately.
She walked along, searching for the darkest
earth that she could find. She found it under a
crabwood tree and knew without a doubt that she
had found the right place. She thrust down her long
finger and deposited the grain of millet, a thousand times small.
Immediately a flower burst forth made of the rarest and most
marvelous shapes and colors. At its heart was the tiniest,
most delicate little girl ever to be seen. The woman
smiled the smile of a mother. She named her
child Thumbelina, so little, so pretty and
so sweet did she appear. The woman ran
across the fields to tell her husband
of the miracle, but he had already left
on a long voyage in search of the
orange-headed tortoise. No one knew
when he would return.
In the meanwhile, Thumbelina
would grow.

Placing Thumbelina in a curl by her ear,
the woman returned home regally adorned.
Her house, however, was no palace.
It was neat and clean, but poor in woven mats
and carved calabash. Taking the shiny shell of a
cashew nut, polished by the sun, the woman made
Thumbelina a large bed, over which she scattered
satiny, perfumed petals. Thumbelina fell into the
deepest of sleeps. The woman's many children were
impatient with curiosity, but also a little frightened,
surprised and full of wonder when they saw their
new sister.
How little she is...
How sweet she seems...
How pretty she is...

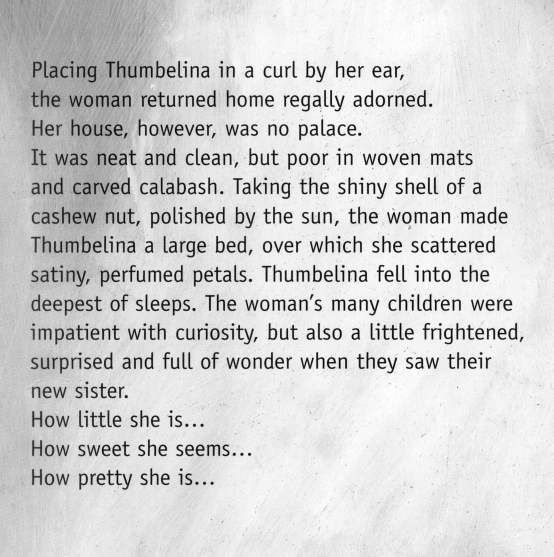

All of her brothers and sisters complimented Thumbelina
except for one who said:
—As for me, I am very hungry. I will chew her up well.
With that, the dreadful idea of eating Thumbelina arose.
But as it turned out, Thumbelina's life took another turn.

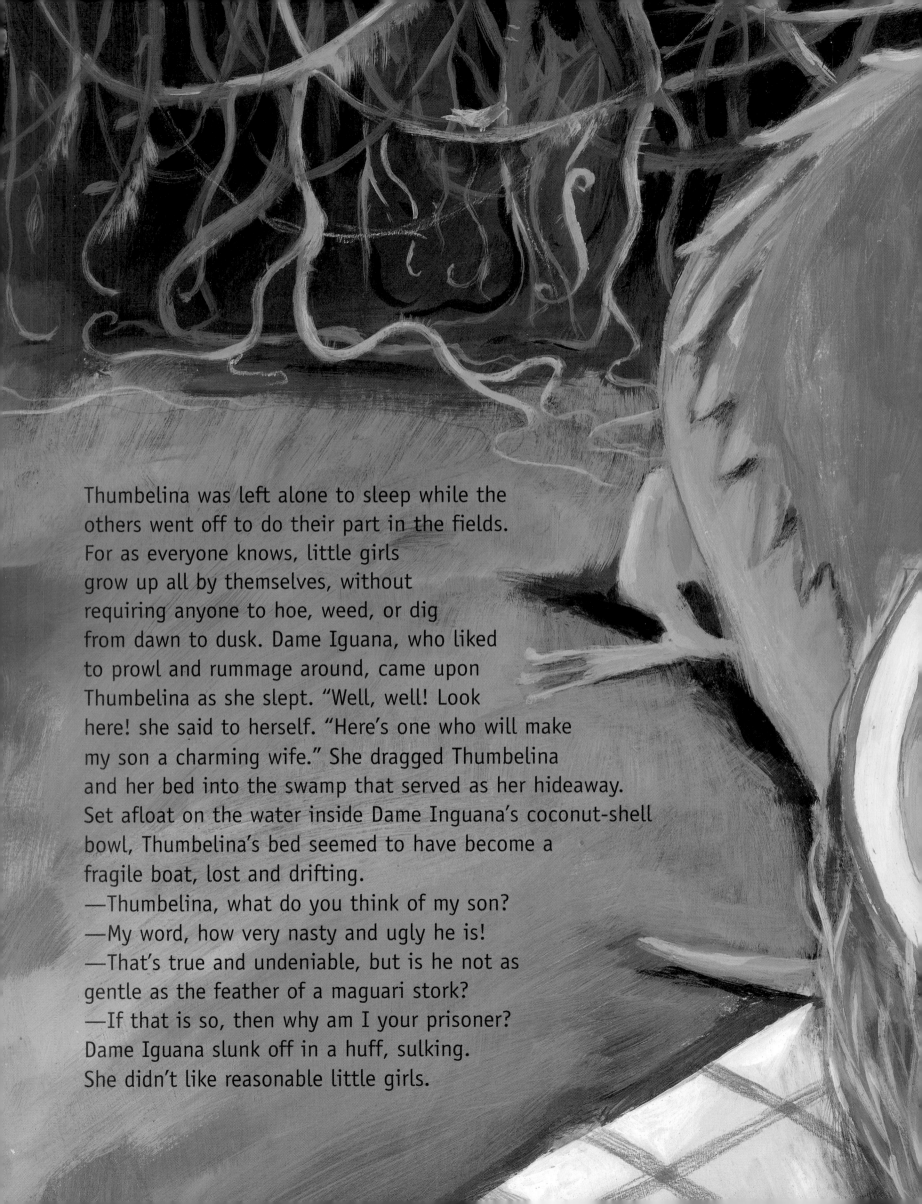

Thumbelina was left alone to sleep while the
others went off to do their part in the fields.
For as everyone knows, little girls
grow up all by themselves, without
requiring anyone to hoe, weed, or dig
from dawn to dusk. Dame Iguana, who liked
to prowl and rummage around, came upon
Thumbelina as she slept. "Well, well! Look
here! she said to herself. "Here's one who will make
my son a charming wife." She dragged Thumbelina
and her bed into the swamp that served as her hideaway.
Set afloat on the water inside Dame Inguana's coconut-shell
bowl, Thumbelina's bed seemed to have become a
fragile boat, lost and drifting.
—Thumbelina, what do you think of my son?
—My word, how very nasty and ugly he is!
—That's true and undeniable, but is he not as
gentle as the feather of a maguari stork?
—If that is so, then why am I your prisoner?
Dame Iguana slunk off in a huff, sulking.
She didn't like reasonable little girls.

Night fell and the iguana family went to sleep amidst a wild
tangle of roots at the edge of the swamp. The animals of the
surrounding area, alerted to this, flew, ran, crawled and
glided over to admire Thumbelina. Ibis, armadillo, ocelot, manatee,
saki monkey, jabiru, canine macaw and tree boa lost confidence
in their own hair, feathers, paws and beaks. Look how small she is!
How sweet! How pretty!
— Do you wish to marry us, Thumbelina?
Thumbelina, who didn't know how to say "yes" or "no," said only:
— Fish! Fish! Fish!

At these words, whoever was
lucky enough to be wearing scales,
jumped, gulped, and carried off
Thumbelina, saving her from the
lovesick animals, a true peril. For if one love
is worth one hundred dangers, the worst of
dangers is to accumulate one thousand loves.

The tall, deep forest, home
to neither jaguarundi nor coral snake,
sheltered Thumbelina. The jealous beetles
with their gleaming coats protected her
while she gathered berries and flowers
along the banks of the melodious river.
—As for myself, I do not wish to marry
you in the least!
It was a blind crab-eating raccoon
that muttered this aloud.
—You are not as pretty as one of our own.
—How do you know?
—I know what I know and do not like
what I do not know. I wish only to
play a game of cards with you.
—I don't know how to play spades,
diamonds, or hearts. Along the river,
I have come upon only club-shaped clover.
—No foolish excuses. Just say "no."
—No!
The crab-eating raccoon left
without another word.
Thumbelina was amazed. How could such a
little *no* achieve such a great thing?

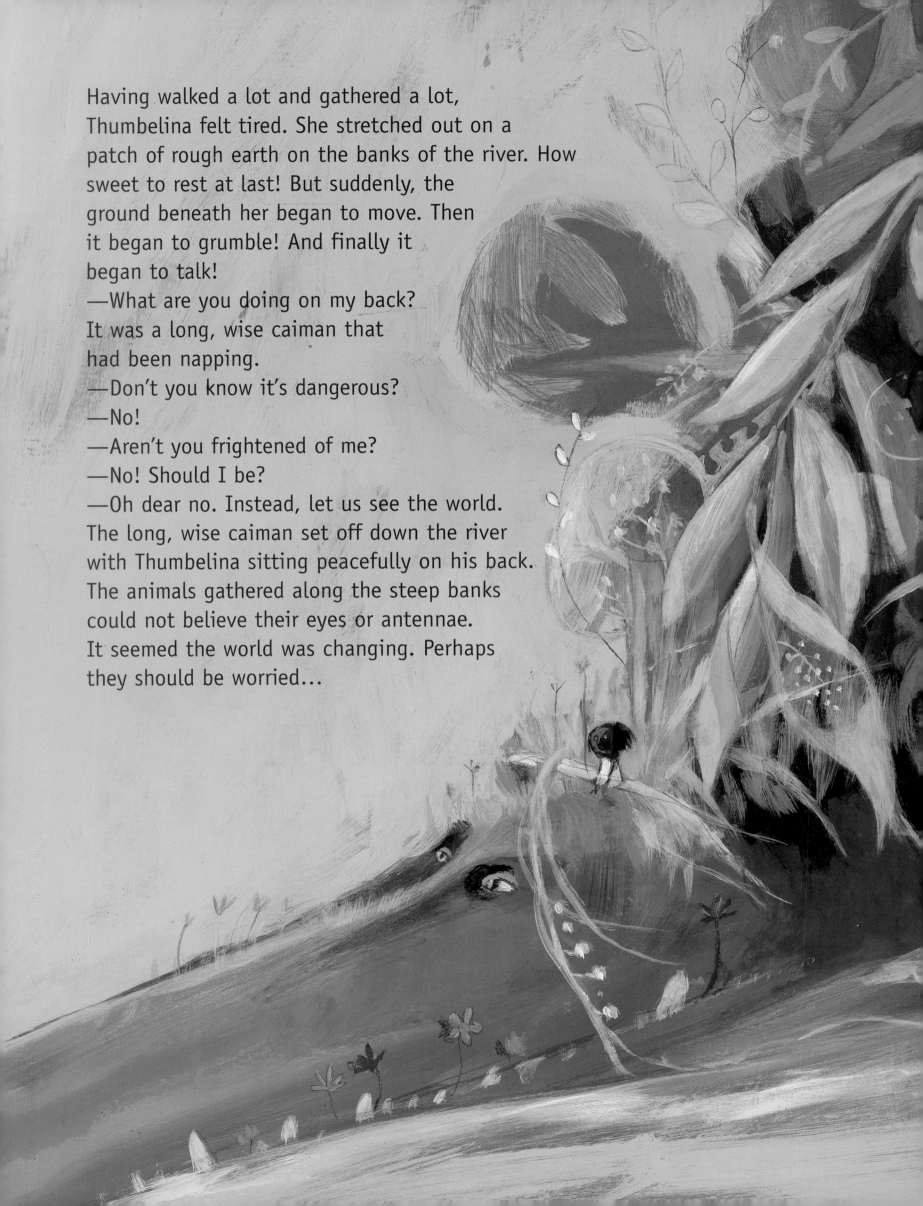

Having walked a lot and gathered a lot,
Thumbelina felt tired. She stretched out on a
patch of rough earth on the banks of the river. How
sweet to rest at last! But suddenly, the
ground beneath her began to move. Then
it began to grumble! And finally it
began to talk!
—What are you doing on my back?
It was a long, wise caiman that
had been napping.
—Don't you know it's dangerous?
—No!
—Aren't you frightened of me?
—No! Should I be?
—Oh dear no. Instead, let us see the world.
The long, wise caiman set off down the river
with Thumbelina sitting peacefully on his back.
The animals gathered along the steep banks
could not believe their eyes or antennae.
It seemed the world was changing. Perhaps
they should be worried...

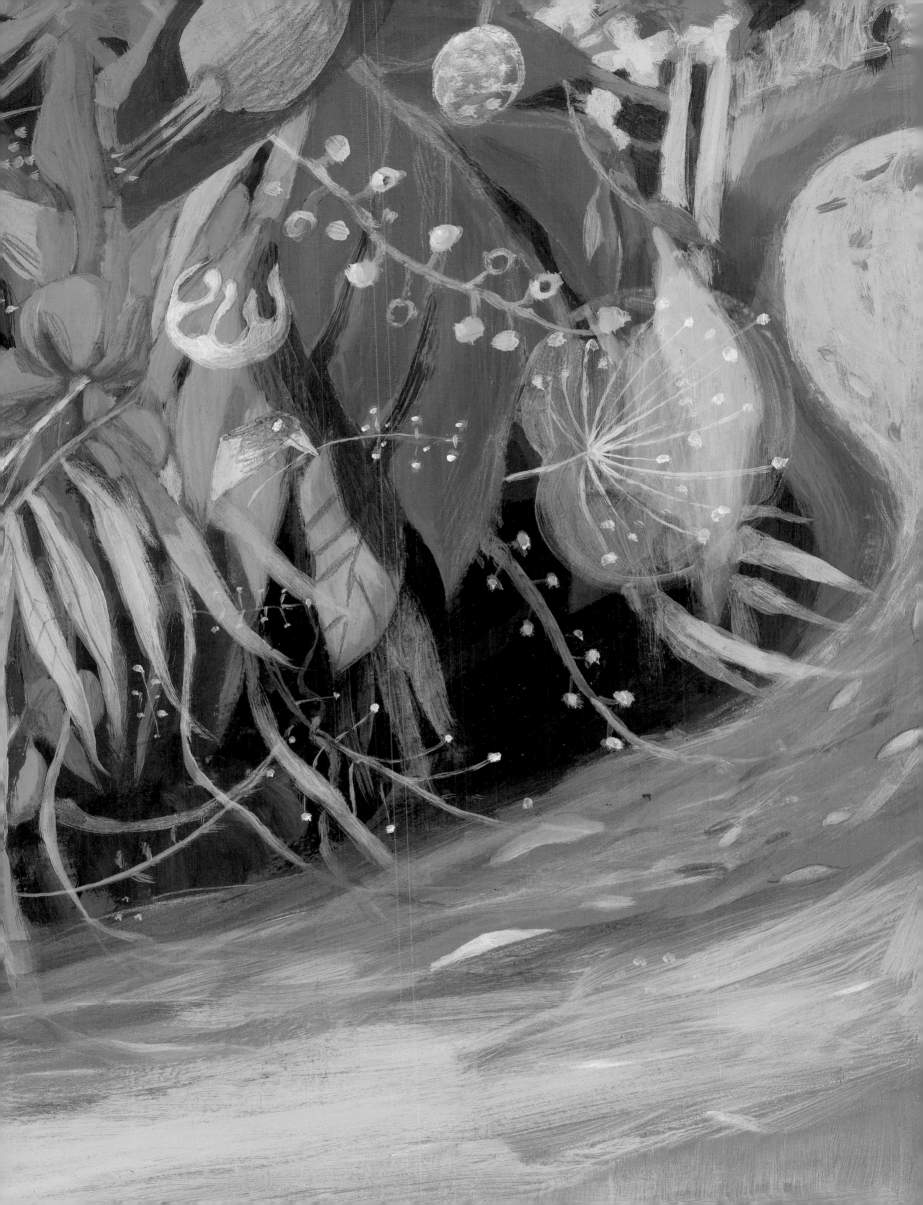

And so it was that
Thumbelina traveled down
the clear, rapid river.
—Have you seen enough
of the wide world? asked
the long, wise caiman.
—I believe so.
—Then it's time to return home.

Thumbelina thanked him and as she said farewell, she grasped
a branch of the wacapou tree that draped over the river as if to
admire itself. As swift and as nimble as only a Tom Thumb or a
Thumbelina can be, she climbed up the proud tree. There she met a
showy, yet slothful sloth. He bragged and boasted about his abundant
riches and about all his friends in zoos throughout the world.
—Thumbelina, you are sprightly and I am slow. You are
courageous and I am lazy. I am rich and you have nothing.
So ask me to marry you.
—Why don't you ask me yourself?
—It's too tiring.
—Then you keep your slothfulness and I'll keep my sweetness.
To Thumbelina this seemed the best choice of all.

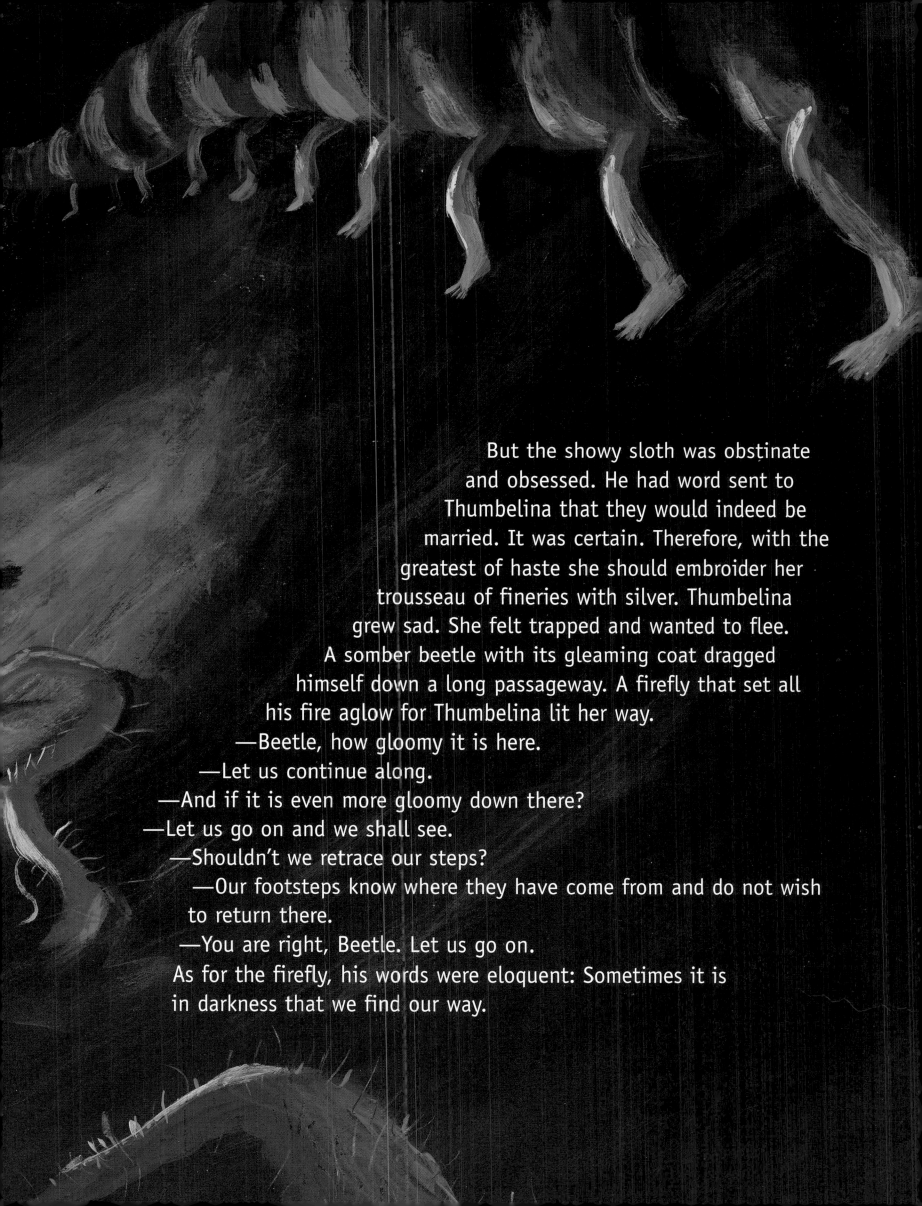

But the showy sloth was obstinate
and obsessed. He had word sent to
Thumbelina that they would indeed be
married. It was certain. Therefore, with the
greatest of haste she should embroider her
trousseau of fineries with silver. Thumbelina
grew sad. She felt trapped and wanted to flee.
A somber beetle with its gleaming coat dragged
himself down a long passageway. A firefly that set all
his fire aglow for Thumbelina lit her way.
—Beetle, how gloomy it is here.
—Let us continue along.
—And if it is even more gloomy down there?
—Let us go on and we shall see.
—Shouldn't we retrace our steps?
—Our footsteps know where they have come from and do not wish
to return there.
—You are right, Beetle. Let us go on.
As for the firefly, his words were eloquent: Sometimes it is
in darkness that we find our way.

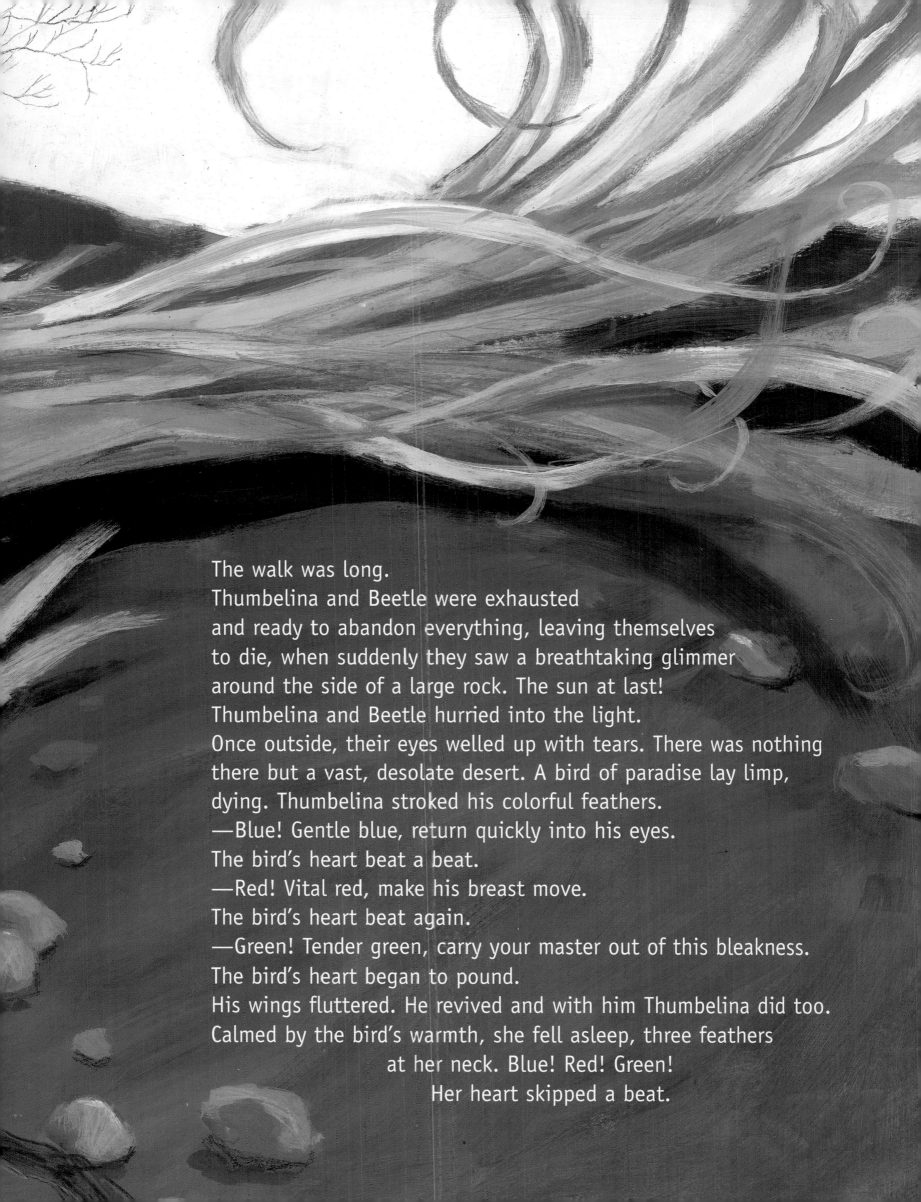

The walk was long.
Thumbelina and Beetle were exhausted
and ready to abandon everything, leaving themselves
to die, when suddenly they saw a breathtaking glimmer
around the side of a large rock. The sun at last!
Thumbelina and Beetle hurried into the light.
Once outside, their eyes welled up with tears. There was nothing
there but a vast, desolate desert. A bird of paradise lay limp,
dying. Thumbelina stroked his colorful feathers.
—Blue! Gentle blue, return quickly into his eyes.
The bird's heart beat a beat.
—Red! Vital red, make his breast move.
The bird's heart beat again.
—Green! Tender green, carry your master out of this bleakness.
The bird's heart began to pound.
His wings fluttered. He revived and with him Thumbelina did too.
Calmed by the bird's warmth, she fell asleep, three feathers
at her neck. Blue! Red! Green!
Her heart skipped a beat.

In the morning when Thumbelina awoke,
the bird of paradise was no longer there.
Thumbelina could only think,
"I save you. You abandon me.
Is that what it means to be free?"
Thumbelina was in despair.
She had no other choice than to return to the
showy sloth and to marry him in a sad ceremony.

Thumbelina looked around.
There was nothing, no one to say goodbye to...
"Except, perhaps, to you," she thought dreamily,
"the stone that marks my path...and to your shadow that
shelters the ant...and to the dust that rises up
under the wind...and to the desert rose that opens
at night when it freezes...and to the tears
that well up in my eyes...." Thumbelina wept.
Her tears were the first water the desert
had tasted in a very long time,
and with them Thumbelina grew wiser,
for it is through such showers of
disappointment that we grow up.

"Thumbelina will marry the sloth!"
The tom-tom beat the news.
Beetle told Toucan the messenger.
Toucan told the bird of paradise, who flew off at full
speed, back to Thumbelina. Up, up, up over
the dense forest he carried her. Down below they
could see the hideous iguana, the showy sloth,
the blind crab-eating raccoon, and the long, wise caiman.
—Thumbelina, what have you learned since you left home?
—To say no.
—What else?
—To beware of riches and to follow in my own footsteps.
—Anything else?
—That the true friend possesses every
color and always returns.
—Do you mean me?
—Yes, I mean you.
The bird of paradise blushed.
In that rosy glow of being loved, all the
colors of the rainbow became one.

The bird of paradise and Thumbelina flew so long
and so far that they arrived in a land of plenty that gave forth
enough for everyone. Tree branches hung heavy with the most colorful,
most juicy, and most fragrant fruits. One had only to stretch out an arm
and open the mouth. The earth was warm and welcoming.
The smallest seed dropped and immediately it would become a guava tree,
or a lemon tree, or a banana tree, thrust fully into flower.
Thumbelina felt content. A pearly rain came to refresh her.
She took cover in a white flower with long, graceful petals.
The bird of paradise rested while keeping watch over her.
Everything was as calm and as peaceful as the
melodious music of the ancient gods.
At last! Such happiness
needs few words.
It breathes.

—Who are you?

Thumbelina was awakened by a gentle yet firm
voice. She opened her eyes. "It's impossible!" she said
to herself. She gazed out at the boy hovering before her,
who could almost have been her reflection
in the river.

—Well, who *are* you?

—And you? asked Thumbelina.

—I am the Spirit of the Flowers.

—The flowers have need of a Spirit?

—If not, then how could they have form,
color and scent all at the same time?

—What do you do?

—I whisper to them, stroke them, and play
music for them in thanks.

—In thanks for what?

—For being beautiful.

—Will you play music for me?

—Once you've become a flower.

—...and I've become beautiful?

—You already are that! In fact, much
too much so to be called Thumbelina.
I will change your name.

Thumbelina felt a shiver
in her heart.
Would such a thing be right?

Thumbelina was troubled.
"Is a garden really where I should live?"
Her heart led her to think about her mother, far off
in a faraway land. "Oh mother, have you grown old?"
And about her brothers and sisters, the old sorcerer,
and the seeds of the twelve lemons.
"How quickly a lemon tree can spring up!"
Full of questions, she wondered, "What should I do now?
Where should I live? Do I go home?"
Toucan the messenger brought her the worn wings
of an old dragonfly that had departed above the clouds.
With them on Thumbelina could fly, which seemed just right!
In an instant they became part of her and she flew!
Toward here or Toulaba?
No one will ever know to which flower
in the infinite garden of possibilities her wings carried her.
Except, perhaps, a dear bird,
who will keep her secret forever.

Glossary of the Exotic

ARMADILLO These are omnivorous, burrowing mammals most closely related to sloths and anteaters. They originated in South America around 50,000,000 years ago. Twenty different species exist, all of which have shells of jointed bony plates covering their backs. Most also have bony rings or plates that protect their long tails. They eat a wide variety of food, including carrion, insects and plants. Found primarily in South America and southwest in the US, they can range as far west as Colorado and as far north as Nebraska. Similar to sloths and anteaters, armadillos are built to dig. Their short legs are both fast and strong, and they have super strong claws.

BIRD OF PARADISE Native to New Guinea and adjacent areas, these birds usually have brilliant plumage and long tail feathers in the male. Many species have elaborate feathers extending from tail, wings and head. In size they range from 1 1/2 ounces and 6 inches to 8 1/2 ounces and 43 inches. While their basic diet consists of insects and spiders, a few species gather nectar and eat frogs and lizards.

CAIMAN or **CAYMAN** Any member of several species of reptiles found in Central and South America, Guyana, French Guiana, Suriname, Tobago and Trinidad. Like alligators, crocodiles, and gavials, caimans are amphibious, lizard-like carnivores. While the young eat a variety of aquatic invertebrates, including insects, crustaceans and mollusks, they eat more and more vertebrates, such as fish, amphibians, reptiles, and water birds as they grow up. Adults might even eat mammalian prey. They live along the edges of rivers and other bodies of water, and grow to a length of 4-7 feet.

CALABASH This tree grows in Central and South America, the West Indies, and far to the south in Florida. It produces large, spherical fruits, up to 20 inches in diameter, the hard-shells of which are often ornamentally carved and used for bowls, ladles, and cups when hollowed out.

CANINE MACAW This is the common name for about 18 species of large colorful parrots native to Central and tropical South America and Mexico. The males and females look alike, which is uncommon among brightly-colored birds. Most species inhabit rainforest areas, but some prefer woodland and savanna-like habitats. While size and color vary, all are vivid, with large, powerful hook-shaped beaks and long tails. They feed on fruit, nuts and seeds, and nest in holes in cliffs and trees. While many species are named after the color of their plumage, the canine macaw is named for the sharpness of its beak.

CORAL SNAKE These venomous snakes are striking for their red, yellow and black bands of color. They have small fangs on their top jaw that deliver their venom. They are not aggressive, however, and bites usually occur by accident. Most species are small (just under two feet long), with thin bodies, small heads, small eyes, and a rounded snout. These snakes spend most of their time underground in cracks or crevices or burrowing in leaves, so they seldom are seen. They also are nocturnal. Different species are found all over the world, but no matter where they live, they subsist on small lizards, other snakes, reptiles and amphibians.

CRAB-EATING RACCOON This is a species of raccoon native to the marshy jungle areas of Central and South America. Resembling the Common Raccoon of North America with its bushy ringed tail and black-masked eyes, it has shorter fur of a brown or grayish-brown color and is larger in size. Its diet consists of frogs, toads, crabs, shrimps, turtle eggs, fruits, and seeds. In terms of personality, this raccoon is solitary and nocturnal.

CRABWOOD TREE or **ANDIROBA** This tree belongs to the mahogany family. The several species of crabwood that exist are all medium-sized to large trees, the largest reaching 100 feet tall. They are found in tropical South America and Africa. The wood of this tree is highly prized for its strength and the oil produced from its seeds is prized for use on the skin.

IBIS Medium to large in size, these are wading and terrestrial birds with a long, downward-curving bill, perfect for probing in mud for crustaceans or for finding and eating grasshoppers, beetles, worms, fish and carrion. Related to both storks and spoonbills, they tend to feed as a group and to nest in trees, bushes and on cliff sides near water. Their long legs and toes make them comfortable walking, flying and perching. They inhabit all continents except Antarctica and live in diverse habitats, such as wetlands, forests, savannas, and costal areas.

IGUANA Any of various large tropical American lizards with spiny projections along their backs. They live in tropical rainforest areas and spend most of their time 40-50 feet above ground in the forest canopy. They have sharp claws for climbing trees, but also are very quick on their feet and are excellent swimmers. Although they are omnivores, they mostly eat plants, leaves and fruits. Iguana young will eat eggs, insects and other smaller vertebrates.

JABIRU This large stork is one of the largest flying birds in the world, and one of the most graceful. Found in the Americas from Mexico to Argentina, it is most common in Brazil and Paraguay. They live in groups near rivers, ponds, and marshy areas, and tend to build their nests atop tall trees. They generally eat large amounts of fish, mollusks, and amphibians, but will eat reptiles, small mammals, fresh carrion, and dead fish. The name "Jabiru" comes from the Tupi-Guaraní language and means "swollen neck," deriving from the inflatable red pouch that both males and females have at the base of the neck. While their plumage is white, their head and neck are featherless and black, except for the lower portion of neck that is pink when they are calm, but turns red with irritation. An adult can reach up to 20 pounds, 4 feet in height, has an 8-foot wingspan and a broad beak a foot long that turns up at the end into a sharp point.

JAGUARUNDI This is a medium-sized wildcat native to Mexico as well as Central and South America. Its average length is just over 4 feet including its tail, which is about 20 inches long. In color they are black, brown or reddish. Among cats, it is most similar to the cougar. Its usual habitat is lowland brush near running water, although it can be found in more tropical areas. Its prey consists of fish, small mammals, reptiles and birds.

MANATEE Sometimes known as sea cows, manatees are fully aquatic, air-breathing sea mammals found mainly in the warm, marshy coastal waters and rivers of the Tropical Americas and Africa. Those that live around Florida have adapted over time to salty water. On average they weigh 900-1200 pounds and are over 10 feet long including their paddle tail, though the females tend to be somewhat larger and heavier than the males. They spend around 12 hours a day asleep in water, but surface regularly for air. They spend the rest of their time grazing in shallow waters for plants to eat. Cousin to the elephant, their large, flexible, prehensile upper lip acts something like a shortened trunk, which they use for foraging, eating, and communicating. It is thought that they use taste, smell, sight, and touch to communicate as well.

MAGUARI STORK This species is found throughout South America. With a height of up to 3 feet, a wingspan of 4 feet and a weight of 7-8 pounds, this stork has mostly white plumage, but black wings and upper tail feathers. It also has a forked tail, a long pointy beak, and unusual eyes, with a creamy white iris and a read stain beneath each eye. Not quite as aquatic as the Jabiru, they live in marshy ground, savanna pounds and lowland areas near sea level. They are omnivores that largely eat frogs, tadpoles, fish, small aquatic rodents, crabs and insects.

OCELOT This is a spotted wildcat found in lowland areas in Central and South America. It also has been spotted in both Trinidad and Texas. It is a brush- and forest-dwelling cat with a tawny-grayish or yellow coat with black spots similar to that of a jaguar. It can grow over 3 feet in length, with a tail over a foot and a half long. When fully grown one can weighs 25-35 pounds. The ocelot is nocturnal, territorial and like most felines largely solitary. For food, it will eat just about any small animal, such as monkeys, snakes, rodents, fish, amphibians, and birds.

ORANGE-HEADED TORTOISE This is so called because of the orange spots it has on its face. It can be found near swampy wetlands, deciduous forest areas, and mountain streams. It

spends much of its time on land hiding in bushes. Geographically, they can be found in Myanmar, Vietnam, Cambodia, Laos, Thailand, Malaysia, and Singapore. While they will eat almost anything, they feed mostly on aquatic plants and fruit.

SAKI MONKEY (or **SAKIS)** These monkeys spend most of their time in trees in the northern and central areas of South America, particularly in Venezuela and Brazil. Their preferred habitat is the tropical rain forest where they can be found as high up as 2,300 feet. Sakis are omnivores, eating fruit, leaves, flowers, honey, insects, small mammals and birds. They also collect bats from tree hollows to eat. In size, the male, at an average weight of 3 1/2 pounds and an average length of 16 inches, with a tail from 12-20 inches, is slightly larger than the female. Sakis have black, grey, or reddish fur depending on the species. The face of some species is naked with the head hooded with fur. The female can have two bright stripes of hair from beneath its eyes extending to mouth or chin.

SLOTH This is a slow-moving mammal, in fact the slowest on earth, that lives in trees and spends most of its life hanging upside down from tree branches. They eat, sleep, mate, and give birth upside down in trees. They hold on to branches with their strong, curved claws. While males are solitary and shy, females sometimes group together. All are nocturnal, though none are what you could ever call active, and all have thick brown coats, and are the size of a domestic cat. They have short, flat heads, big eyes, a short snout, long legs, tiny ears, stubby tails, and are 1 1/2 - 2 feet long. They are largely plant eaters, eating leaves, shoots and fruit, but they also will eat insects, small lizards and carrion.

TOM-TOM Any of various small-headed drums that generally are long and narrow and are beaten with the hands.

TREE BOA While there are many tree-dwelling boas, the name "tree boa" most often refers to seven different species that live mainly in the rain forests of Central and South America, though they can be found in the Virgin Islands and elsewhere. All are long with thin bodies, big heads, big eyes, and huge, elongated front teeth that allow them to firmly grip their primary prey, the birds they hunt and eat. Boas of all seven species are gorgeously colored, with the stunning emerald boa one of the most famous. These snakes are nocturnal, tree dwelling and aggressive, so would not make a good pet.

WACAPOU TREE (*Vouacapoua Americana***)** A tree of very heavy, very solid wood that is nearly impervious to rot. This tree can be found in Surinam, French Guiana, and Brazil in upland forest areas. A canopy tree without a peak with a fluted lower trunk, this tree can grow as tall as 50-75 feet in height.